Fern
the Green
Fairy

To the fairies at the
bottom of my garden

Special thanks to
Narinder Dhami

No part of this publication may be reproduced in whole or in part, or
stored in a retrieval system, or transmitted in any form or by any
means, electronic, mechanical, photocopying, or otherwise, without
written permission of the publisher. For information regarding
permission, write to Rainbow Magic Limited, c/o HIT Entertainment,
830 South Greenville Avenue, Allen, TX 75002-3320.

ISBN-13: 978-0-439-74467-6
ISBN-10: 0-439-74467-9

Text copyright © 2003 by Rainbow Magic Limited.

Illustrations copyright © 2003 by Georgie Ripper.

All rights reserved. Published by Scholastic Inc.,
557 Broadway, New York, NY 10012, by arrangement
with Rainbow Magic Limited.

SCHOLASTIC, LITTLE APPLE, and associated logos are trademarks
and/or registered trademarks of Scholastic Inc.
RAINBOW MAGIC is a trademark of Rainbow Magic Limited. Reg.
U.S. Patent & Trademark Office and other countries. HIT and the
HIT logo are trademarks of HIT Entertainment Limited.

12 11 10 9   10 11 12/0

Printed in China

Fern
the Green
Fairy

by Daisy Meadows
illustrated by Georgie Ripper

SCHOLASTIC INC.

New York   Toronto   London   Auckland   Sydney
Mexico City   New Delhi   Hong Kong   Buenos Aires

The
Fairyland
Palace

Maze

Forest

Orchard

Black
Pot

Meadow

Tower

Beach

Tide pools

Rainspell Island

Shel

Jack Frost's
Ice Castle

Tom Goodfellow's
House

Merry-go-round

Willow
Tree

Mrs. Merry's
Cottage

Stream

Field

Mermaid
Cottage

Town

Harbor

Dolphin Cottage

Cold winds blow and thick ice forms,
I conjure up this fairy storm.
To seven corners of the human world
the Rainbow Fairies will be hurled!

I curse every part of Fairyland,
with a frosty wave of my icy hand.
For now and always, from this day,
Fairyland will be cold and gray!

Ruby, Amber, and Sunny
are out of danger.
Can Rachel and Kirsty free
Fern the Green Fairy, too?

Contents

The Secret Garden

"Oh!" Rachel Walker gasped in delight as she looked around her. "What a perfect place for a picnic!"

"It's a secret garden," Kirsty Tate said, her eyes shining.

The two girls were standing in a large garden. It looked as if nobody else had been there for a long, long time. Pink and

1

white roses grew all around the tree trunks, filling the air with their sweet smell. White marble statues stood here and there, half hidden by green ivy. And right in the middle of the garden was a crumbling stone tower.

"There was a castle here once called Moonspinner Castle," Mr. Walker said, walking up behind them. He was reading from his guidebook. "But now all that's left is the tower."

Rachel and Kirsty stared up at the ruined tower. The yellow stones glowed warmly in the sunshine. They were spotted with soft, green moss. Near the top of the tower was a small, square window.

"It's just like Rapunzel's tower," Kirsty said. "I wonder if we can get up to the top somehow?"

"Let's go see!" Rachel said eagerly. "I want to explore the whole garden. Can we, Mom?"

"Go ahead." Mrs. Walker smiled. "Your dad and I will get the food ready." She opened the picnic basket. "But don't be too long, girls."

Rachel and Kirsty rushed over to the
door in the side of the tower. Kirsty
tugged at the heavy iron handle. But the
door was locked.

Rachel was disappointed. "Oh, that's
too bad," she said.

Kirsty sighed. "Yes, I was hoping Fern
the Green Fairy might be here."

Rachel and Kirsty had a secret. During their vacation on Rainspell Island, they were helping to find the seven Rainbow Fairies. The fairies had been sent out of Fairyland by evil Jack Frost, and Fairyland had lost all its color without them. Fairyland would only be bright and beautiful when all seven fairies returned home again.

"Fern," Rachel called in a low voice. "Are you here?"

Here . . . Here . . . Here . . .

Her words echoed off the stones. Rachel and Kirsty held their breath and waited. But they couldn't hear anything except leaves rustling in the breeze.

"This is such a special place," Kirsty

said. "It *feels* like there's magic close by."
Then she gasped and pointed. "Rachel,
look at the ivy!"

Rachel stared. Glossy green leaves grew
thickly on the wall, but in one place the
stones were bare, in the shape of a perfect
circle.

Rachel's heart began to beat faster. "It

looks just like a fairy ring!" she said. She
had heard that when plants grew in a
circle, it was the work of fairy magic.
Rachel ran around the tower to take a
closer look and almost tripped
over one of her shoelaces.

"Careful!" Kirsty said,
grabbing Rachel's arm.

Rachel sat down on
a mossy stone to retie
her shoe. "There's
green *everywhere*," she
said, looking around
at the thick grass and
the leafy trees. "Fern
must be here."

"We'd better find her
quickly, then," Kirsty said with a shiver.

"Or else Jack Frost's goblins will find her first!"

Jack Frost had sent his goblin servants to Rainspell Island. He wanted them to stop the fairies from getting home to Fairyland. The goblins were so mean that they made everything around them turn cold and icy.

"Where should we start looking?" Rachel asked, standing up again.

Kirsty looked at her friend and

laughed. "You've got green stuff all over you!" she said.

Rachel twisted around to look. The back of her jean skirt was green and dusty. "It must be the moss," she grumbled, brushing it off.

Dust flew up into the air. It sparkled and glittered in the morning sun. As it fell to the ground, tiny green leaves appeared and the smell of freshly cut grass filled the air.

Rachel and Kirsty turned to each other. "It's fairy dust!" they cried together.

Where Is Fern?

"Fern *is* here!" said Kirsty.

"Thank goodness I sat down on that fairy dust!" Rachel said.

The girls walked all around the tower, looking under bushes and inside sweet-smelling flowers. As they walked, they softly called Fern's name. But the Green Fairy was nowhere to be found.

11

"You don't think the goblins have already caught her, do you?" Rachel asked. She was worried.

"I hope not," replied Kirsty. "I'm sure Fern *was* here, but now it seems like she's somewhere else."

"Yes, but where?" Rachel looked around the garden helplessly.

"Maybe there's magic around to help us," Kirsty said.

She looked down at the tiny leaves. Some of them fluttered across the garden. "I know, let's follow the fairy dust!"

The bright green leaves floated over to a narrow path. The path led into a beautiful orchard. Rachel could see apples, pears, and plums growing on the trees.

"It's a magic trail!" Kirsty breathed.

"Quick, let's keep following the fairy dust," Rachel said.

Rachel and Kirsty set off down the path, which twisted and turned through the fruit trees.

Suddenly, the path led them into a large clearing. Kirsty's eyes opened wide when she saw what was in front of them. "It's a maze!" she cried.

The thick, green hedges loomed above them, their leaves rustling in the breeze.

Rachel nudged Kirsty. "Look!" She pointed. "The fairy trail leads right into the maze!"

"We'll have to take that path," Kirsty said bravely.

The two girls followed the floating fairy leaves through the narrow maze entrance. Kirsty felt a little bit scared as the fairy dust led them one way, then another. What if the trail ran out and they got lost in the maze?

"Maybe there will be another clue in

the middle of the maze," Rachel said
hopefully.

"Or maybe Fern will be there!" Kirsty
added.

They turned one more corner and,
suddenly, the hedges parted to reveal the
middle of the maze.
An oak tree stood
in the very center. The
fairy dust led right to
the bottom of the tree,
then stopped.
"Fern must be
here!" Rachel said
excitedly.

Kirsty frowned.
"Yes, but *where*?" she asked, looking
around.

Tap! Tap! Tap!

The two girls jumped.

"What was that?" Rachel gasped.

There it was again. *Tap! Tap! Tap!*

Kirsty's eyes opened wide. "It's coming from over there." She pointed to the oak tree.

"I hope it isn't a trap set by the goblins," Rachel whispered.

Tap! Tap! Tap!

The noise was louder now. Slowly, Rachel and Kirsty walked around the tree. At first, they didn't see anything unusual.

Then Rachel pointed at the tree trunk. "What's a *window* doing in a *tree*?" she asked.

There was a small, hollow knot halfway up the trunk — and it was covered by a glass window!

Kirsty put out her hand and touched the window. It was very cold and wet. "It's not glass," she whispered. "It's *ice*!"

Both girls looked more closely.
Suddenly, something moved behind the
icy window. Kirsty could just barely see a
tiny girl dressed in glittering green.

"Rachel, we've found her!" she said
happily. "It's Fern the Green Fairy!"

Lost in the Maze

Fern waved to the girls through the sheet of ice. Her mouth opened and closed, but Rachel and Kirsty couldn't hear a word she was saying. The ice was too thick.

Rachel looked worried. "Fern must be freezing in there," she said. "We've got to get her out."

21

"We could smash the ice with a stick," said Kirsty. Then she frowned. "But Fern might get hurt."

Rachel thought hard. "We could *melt* the ice," she said.

"How?" Kirsty asked.

"Like this," Rachel replied. She reached up and pressed her hand firmly against the window of ice. Kirsty did the same. The ice felt freezing cold, but they kept pressing against it with their warm hands.

Soon, a few drops of water began to trickle down the window.

"It's melting!" Rachel said. "I think we can make a hole in it now." She gently poked the middle of the window with her finger, and the ice began to crack.

"Don't worry, Fern," said Kirsty. "You'll be out of there very soon!"

There was a sudden crack as the ice split open. A flash of sparkling fairy dust shot out, leaving behind the smell of cut grass. And then Fern the Green Fairy pushed her way out of the tree trunk, her wings fluttering limply. She wore a bright green top and stretchy pants, with pretty leaf shapes around her waist and neck. She had small acorn-colored boots on her tiny feet, earrings, and a pendant that looked like a little green leaf. Her long, brown hair was tied in pigtails, and her thin, emerald wand was tipped with gold.

"Oh, I'm s-s-so c-c-cold!" the fairy gasped, shivering all over. She floated down to rest on Kirsty's shoulder.

"Let me warm you up a bit," said Rachel. She scooped the fairy up and held her in her cupped hands. Then she blew gently on her.

The warmth of Rachel's breath seemed to do the trick. Fern stopped shivering, and her wings straightened out. "Thank you," she said. "I feel much better now."

"I'm Rachel and this is Kirsty," Rachel explained. "We're here to take you to the pot at the end of the rainbow."

"Ruby, Amber, and Sunny are waiting for you," Kirsty added.

Fern's green eyes lit up. "They're safe?" she exclaimed. "That's wonderful!" She flew off Rachel's hand in a burst of green fairy dust and twirled happily in the air. "But what about my other sisters?"

"Don't worry, we're going to find them, too," Kirsty told her. "But how did you get stuck behind that ice window?"

"When I landed on Rainspell Island, I got tangled up in the ivy on the tower," Fern explained. "I managed to untangle myself, but then Jack Frost's goblins started chasing me. So I flew into the maze and hid in the oak tree. It was raining, and when the goblins passed by, their evil magic turned the rainwater to ice. So I was trapped."

Suddenly, Rachel shivered. "It's getting colder," she said. She glanced up at the sky. The sun had disappeared behind a cloud, and there was a sudden chill in the air.

"The goblins might be close by!" Kirsty gasped, looking scared.

Fern nodded. "Yes, we'd better get out of this garden right away," she said calmly. "You know the way, don't you?"

Rachel and Kirsty looked at each other.

"I'm not sure," Kirsty said with a frown. "Do *you* know, Rachel?"

Rachel shook her head. "No," she replied. "But we can follow the fairy trail back to the beginning of the maze."

Kirsty looked around. "Where *is* the fairy trail?" she asked.

An icy breeze was blowing all around them now. The green fairy leaves were drifting away and disappearing.

"Oh, no!" Kirsty cried. "What are we going to do now?"

Suddenly, they heard the sound of heavy footsteps coming through the maze toward them.

"I know that fairy is in here *somewhere*," grumbled a loud, gruff voice.

Fern, Rachel, and Kirsty looked at one another with wide eyes.

"Goblins!" whispered Rachel.

Fairy Fireworks

Rachel, Kirsty, and Fern listened in
horror as the goblins came closer. As
usual, they were arguing with each other.

"Come on!" snorted one goblin. "We
can't let her get away again."

"Stop bossing me around," grumbled
the other one. "I'm going as fast as I
can. OW!"

Just then, there was a loud *THUD*! It sounded like someone had fallen over.

"If your feet weren't so big, you wouldn't trip over them," jeered the first goblin.

"They're big enough to give you a good kick!" the other goblin snapped.

"Let's hide in the tree," Fern whispered to Rachel and Kirsty. "I'll make you fairy-sized so we can all fit under a leaf." Quickly, she shot up into the air and sprinkled the girls with fairy dust. Rachel and Kirsty gasped as they felt themselves shrinking, down and down. It was so exciting!

Once they were small enough, Fern took the girls' hands. "Let's go," she said,

and the three of them fluttered up into
the air and landed on a branch. Fat
brown acorns grew on the tree, as big as
beach balls. Even the thinnest twigs
looked like tree trunks to the tiny girls!

Fern lifted up the edge of a leaf, which
was as big as a tablecloth, and all three
of them crept underneath.

A moment later, the goblins rushed into the clearing.

"Where can that fairy be?" one of them grumbled. "I know she came this way!"

They began to search around the bottom of the tree.

"How are we going to get back to the pot?" Rachel whispered to Fern. "Kirsty and I aren't very good at flying. The goblins will catch us if we try!"

Fern laughed. "Don't worry! I think I

know someone who can help us." She
pointed behind them.

Rachel and Kirsty turned to look.
A gray, furry face was peeking shyly
around the tree trunk. It was a squirrel.

"Hello," Fern called softly.

The squirrel jumped and hid behind the
trunk. Then he peeked out again, his dark
eyes curious.

"Maybe he'd like an acorn,"
Kirsty suggested.

There was a big, shiny
nut growing right next
to her. She wrapped
her arms around it,
but she couldn't pull it
off the twig. It was too
big! Rachel and Fern
came to help. All three of

them tugged at the acorn until it came
off the branch with a crack.

Fern held the acorn out to the squirrel.
"Mmm, a yummy nut!" she said.

The squirrel ran lightly along the
branch, his long, furry tail waving.
He took the acorn and held it in his
front paws.

"What's your name?" asked Fern kindly.

"I'm Fluffy," squeaked the squirrel, between nibbles.

"I'm Fern," said the fairy. "And these are my friends Rachel and Kirsty. We need to get away from the goblins. Will you help us?"

Fluffy shivered. "I don't like goblins," he squeaked.

"We won't let them hurt you," Fern promised, stroking his head. "Can you give us a ride on your back? You can jump from hedge to hedge much better than we can! We have to get out of this maze."

"Yes, I'll help you,"

Fluffy agreed, finishing the last piece of
his acorn.

Rachel, Kirsty, and Fern climbed
onto the squirrel's back. Kirsty thought
it felt like sinking into a big, soft
blanket.

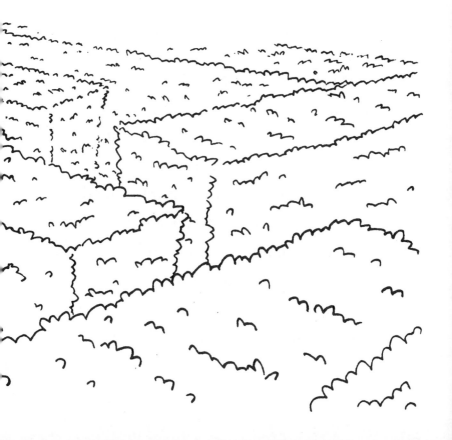

"This is great," said Fern, snuggling
down into the squirrel's fur. "Let's go,
Fluffy!"

The squirrel turned and ran along the
branch. Rachel, Kirsty, and Fern clung
tightly to Fluffy's thick fur as he jumped

out of the tree, right over the goblins' heads! He landed on the closest hedge. The goblins were so busy arguing, they didn't even notice.

Fern leaned forward to whisper in the squirrel's ear. "Well done, Fluffy. Now, the next one!"

Rachel gulped when she saw how far away the next hedge was. "Maybe Fluffy needs some fairy magic to help him," she said.

"No, he doesn't," Fern replied, her green eyes twinkling. "He'll be fine!"

Fluffy leaped into midair. He sailed across the gap and landed safely on top of the next hedge. Rachel and Kirsty grinned at each other. This was so exciting! It was a bit bumpy, but Fluffy's fur was like a soft cushion. The squirrel was moving so fast, it wasn't long before they had left the goblins far behind.

"We made it!" Fern said at last, as Fluffy reached the edge of the maze. "Now, which way do we go, girls?"

Rachel and Kirsty looked at each other in dismay. "This isn't how we came *in*,"

Rachel said. "I don't know the way
back to the pot from here. Do you,
Kirsty?"

Kirsty shook her head.

Fern looked worried. "But I have to get
back to the pot!" she said. "That's where
my sisters are!"

"Oh!" Kirsty had an idea. "Rachel,
what about looking in our magic bags
for help?"

"Good idea," Rachel agreed.

Titania, the Fairy Queen, had given
Rachel and Kirsty two special magic
bags, for whenever they needed help
rescuing the fairies. The girls took the
bags with them everywhere, just in case.

Kirsty opened her backpack and looked
inside. One of the magic bags was
glowing with a silvery light. "I wonder
what's inside," she said, reaching in.

She pulled out a thin, green stick covered with sparkling gold stars.

"It looks like a *sparkler*," Rachel said. "That's not much use, is it?"

"It's a fairy sparkler!" said Fern excitedly. "I can use it to write a message in the sky, and my sisters will see it from the pot. Then they'll know we need help."

"But what about the goblins?" Rachel asked. "Won't they see it, too, and know where we are?"

Fern looked serious. "We've got to take the risk," she said. Fern held the sparkler in one hand, her wings fluttering. She lit the top with her wand and quickly flew up into the sky.

Rachel and Kirsty held their breath. Fern and the sparkler shot upward, trailing bright green sparks behind them. Fern flew higher and higher into the sky, and used the sparkler to write a message in a shower of emerald stars. The stars spelled out the words:

HELP WE'RE LOST

They twinkled brightly in the
darkening sky before fading away.

"We won't have to wait long," Fern
said, landing beside Rachel and Kirsty on
the ground. "Help will come very soon."

Rachel and Kirsty wondered what
would happen. How could the fairies
come to their rescue? They weren't

supposed to leave the pot at the end of the
rainbow, in case the goblins found them.
Suddenly, the leaves behind Rachel,
Kirsty, and Fern rustled.

"Did you see the fairy sparkler?"
shouted a loud goblin voice. "It came
from over there. Quick, before that fairy
gets away again!"

Hedgehog Help

Rachel and Kirsty looked at each other in alarm. Fluffy seemed scared, too. The goblins were on their trail again!

"They're coming toward us," Rachel whispered as the goblin voices got louder.

"Don't worry," Fern said, smiling. She didn't seem nervous. "My sisters will send help quickly."

Just then, Rachel spotted a line of golden sparkles twinkling toward them through the fruit trees. "What's that?" she whispered.

"Is it goblin magic?" Kirsty asked, suspicious.

Fern shook her head. "They're fireflies! My sisters must have sent them to show us the way back to the pot."

Suddenly, there was another shout from inside the maze. "Look, what are those lights over there?"

"The goblins have spotted the fireflies!" Rachel gasped.

"Quickly, Fluffy!" Fern said as they all climbed onto the squirrel's back again. "Follow the fireflies!"

The golden specks were dancing away through the trees. Fluffy scampered after them, just as the goblins dashed out of the maze.

"There's the fairy!" one of them shouted, pointing at Fern. "Stop that squirrel!"

"Come back!" the other roared as Fluffy ran off.

Rachel, Kirsty, and Fern
clung to Fluffy's fur as the
squirrel zigzagged back
and forth to get away
from the goblins.
Fluffy scrambled
up the trunk of the
nearest tree. He was
just about to jump across
to the next, when someone
called to them from below.

"Hello!"

"Who's that?" Rachel asked. She,
Kirsty, and Fern peered
down at the ground.
A hedgehog was
standing at the foot of
the apple tree. "Hello!"
he hollered again.

"The animals in the garden have heard that you're in trouble. We'd like to help."

"Oh, thank you!" Fern called. Then she gasped as the two goblins appeared among the trees.

"Where'd that squirrel go?" one of them yelled.

Quickly, Fluffy leaped across to the next apple tree. The goblins roared with anger and dashed forward. At that moment, the hedgehog curled himself into a ball and rolled right into their path. Rachel thought he looked like a big, prickly soccer ball.

"OW!" both goblins howled. "My toes!"

Rachel and Kirsty couldn't help laughing as the goblins jumped around holding their feet. "Hooray for Hedgehog!" the girls shouted.

As Fluffy jumped from one fruit tree to

the next, the firefly lights behind them began to go out.

"Hey! Who turned off the lights?" wailed one of the goblins, still rubbing his foot. "Which way are we supposed to go?"

"How should I know?" snapped the other goblin. Their voices were getting fainter now as Fluffy hurried on.

"Thank you, fireflies!" called Fern, waving at the last few specks of light. "We need to find our way to the orchard wall from here. We can't be far from the pot now."

"If I were human-sized, I

could probably figure out which way to go," Kirsty said. "But everything looks so big and unfamiliar!"

"But if we go back to our normal sizes, the goblins will surely spot us!" said Rachel.

"I can help you," a small voice whispered. A fawn was standing at the bottom of the tree. Her golden brown coat was short and silky, and she stared up at them with big, brown eyes.

"You mean you can show us the way?" Kirsty said.

"Yes, I can." The deer nodded, twitching her little tail. "I can show you a shortcut."

She trotted off through the trees on her long legs. Fluffy followed her, leaping from branch to branch above the little deer's head.

Rachel was so excited she could hardly breathe. She was riding on a squirrel's back, being shown the way to the pot at the end of the rainbow by a fawn!

A few moments later, they reached the brick wall that ran around the outside of the orchard. Fluffy leaped up to the top of the wall, and Rachel and Kirsty looked eagerly ahead of them. On the other side of the wall was a meadow, and beyond that was a patch of woods.

"Look!" Rachel shouted. "That's where the pot is!"

Flying High

"Thank you!" Kirsty and Rachel called to the baby deer. She blinked her long eyelashes at them and trotted away.

A blackbird with shiny, dark feathers was sitting on the wall nearby. He hopped over to them. "I'm here to take you to the pot at the end of the rainbow," he chirped. "All aboard!"

Fluffy looked sad as Fern, Rachel, and Kirsty slid off his back and climbed onto the blackbird. It was a tight squeeze, and the bird's feathers felt smooth and silky after Fluffy's thick fur.

"Good-bye, Fluffy!" called Rachel. She blew him a kiss. "And thank you!" She felt sad to leave their new

friend behind. Then the blackbird soared
into the air.

"Look for the big weeping willow tree,"
Rachel told the blackbird as he swooped
over the meadow.

"I can't wait to see my sisters again,"
said Fern, sounding very excited.

The blackbird flew over the woods and

landed in the clearing near the willow tree. Rachel, Kirsty, and Fern jumped down onto the grass, calling good-bye to the blackbird.

"Who's there?" croaked a stern voice. A plump, green frog hopped out from under the hanging branches of the tree.

"Bertram, it's me!" Fern called. Quickly, the fairy waved her wand, and Rachel and Kirsty shot up to their normal size again.

"Miss Fern!" Bertram said joyfully. "You're back!"

"We followed the fireflies," Fern said, giving the frog a hug. "Thank you for sending them."

"We saw the sparkler in the sky,"
Bertram explained, "so we knew you
were in trouble. But you'll be safe here,"
he went on. "The pot is hidden under
the tree. The goblins have no idea that
it's here!"

Rachel and Kirsty hurried over and
pulled aside the long branches. The pot at
the end of the rainbow lay there on its side.

Suddenly, a fountain of red, orange, and
yellow fairy dust whooshed out of the
pot. Ruby, Amber, and Sunny flew out,

looking very excited. A big queen bee
buzzed out behind them.

"Fern!" Ruby called. "You're safe! It's so
good to see you!"

Rachel and Kirsty beamed as they
watched the fairies hug one another. The
air around them fizzed and popped with

red flowers, orange bubbles, yellow butterflies, and green leaves.

"We really missed you," said Sunny. The bee nudged her with a tiny feeler. "Oh, sorry, Queenie," said Sunny. "This is my sister Fern."

Queenie buzzed, "Hello!"

"How did you get back so quickly?" asked Amber. "We sent the fireflies only a little while ago."

"Our forest friends helped us," Fern said. She waved as the blackbird flew off. "Especially Fluffy the squirrel." She sighed. "It was sad to leave him behind."

Ruby laughed. "Who's that, then?" she asked, pointing at a tree on the other side of the clearing.

Rachel and Kirsty looked, too. Fluffy was peeking at them from behind the tree trunk, looking very shy.

"Fluffy!" Fern flew over and hugged him. "What are you doing here?"

"I was worried about you," Fluffy explained shyly. "I wanted to make sure you got back to the pot safely."

"Would you like to stay with us, too?" asked Amber. "You could live in the willow tree, couldn't you?"

"Yes, *please*," squeaked Fluffy. "I'm very

lonely. I live in that oak tree inside the maze all by myself!"

Ruby turned to Rachel and Kirsty. "Thank you again," she said. "I don't know what we'd do without you!"

Fern fluttered lightly onto Rachel's shoulder. One of her wings brushed softly against Rachel's cheek, like a butterfly. "We'll see you again soon, won't we?"

"Yes, of course," Rachel promised.

"Only three more Rainbow Fairies left to find!" Kirsty added. She took Rachel's hand and they waved to the fairies, then ran out of the clearing. "We'd better get back to your mom and dad, Rachel. They'll be wondering where we are."

"Good idea." Rachel laughed. "If we don't hurry back, my dad will eat the whole picnic by himself!"

THE RAINBOW FAIRIES

Ruby, Amber, Sunny, and Fern are safe.
Now Rachel and Kirsty must look for

Sky the Blue Fairy!

But where could she be? Follow along
with Rachel and Kirsty in this special
sneak peek. . . .

A Magic Messenger

"The water's really warm!" Rachel Walker laughed. She was sitting on a rock, swishing her toes in one of Rainspell Island's deep blue tide pools. Her friend Kirsty Tate was looking for shells nearby.

"Be careful not to slip, Kirsty!" called

Mrs. Tate. She was sitting farther down the beach with Mrs. Walker.

"OK, Mom!" Kirsty yelled back. As she looked down at her bare feet, a patch of green seaweed began to move. There was something blue and shiny underneath it. "Rachel! Come here," she shouted.

Rachel went over to Kirsty. "What is it?" she asked.

Kirsty pointed to the seaweed.

"There's something blue under there," she said. "I wonder, could it be . . ."

"Sky the Blue Fairy?" Rachel said eagerly.

Jack Frost had banished the seven Rainbow Fairies from Fairyland with a magic spell. Now they were hidden all over Rainspell Island. Until they were all found, there would be no color in